Ptolemy Turtle

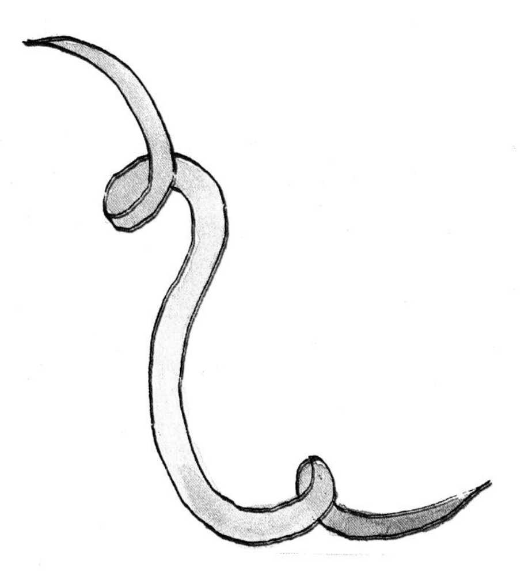

Ptolemy Turtle

Written and illustrated by
Mélisande Potter-Hall

10987654321

Published by: LMH Publishing Limited
7 Norman Road,
LOJ Industrial Complex
Building 10
Kingston C.S.O., Jamaica

E-mail: lmhpublishing@cwjamaica.com
Fax: 928-8036

ISBN: 976-610-172-8

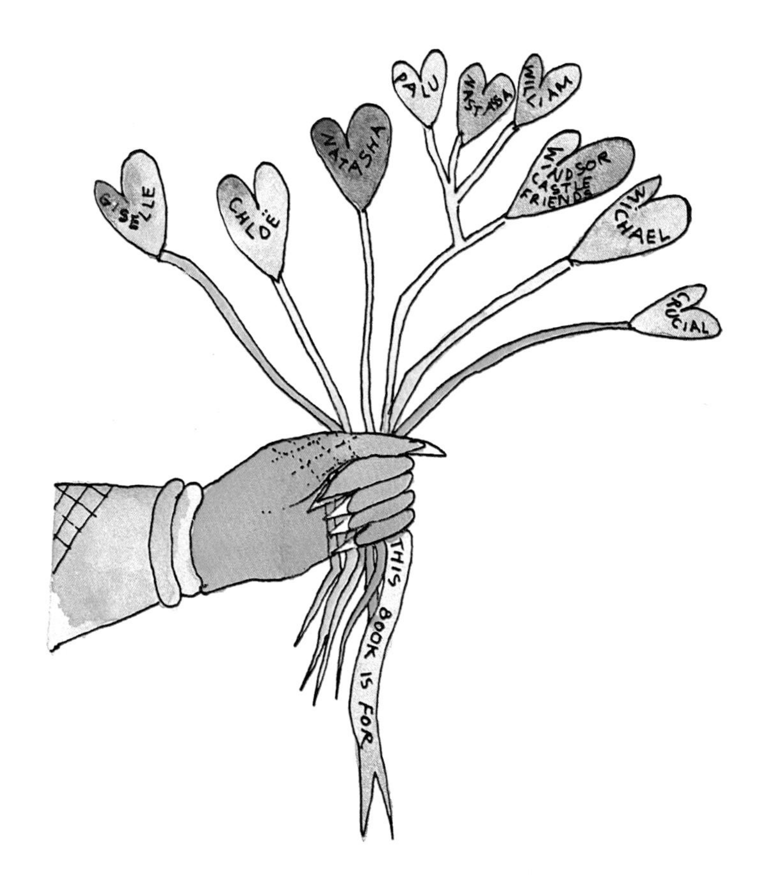

My special thanks to:
Laura-Lee Fields, who supports the arts.
Eva Myers, Evita's Restaurant, Ocho Rios.
James Merrill, Poet Laureate.
Kim Robinson-Walcott, Editorial Director, Kingston Publishers.
Chloë and Giselle, my daughters.

A Close-up of Ptolemy

Ptolemy Turtle lived on the edge of the White River under a heavenly allspice tree. There his mother, Mummy Turtle, taught him many facts; politeness and how to reason. He knew how many eggs equal a dozen, the best technique for catching parrot fish and when to say "Mornin'" and "Evenin'."

Mummy Turtle

Blue Drawers

Still Ptolemy had a reputation in his neighbourhood for being a spoiled turtle, for his mother loved him so dearly, she would do anything under the sun to see him happy. When Ptolemy wanted coconut cookies or blue drawers, sweet Mummy would get out her well-used pot and seastone which she used as a rolling pin.

If he was thirsty she would pound chocolate beans to make him hot chocolate tea. If he was ailing with a sore throat she would boil a green tea of cerasee and devil's horsewhip to soothe his larynx. If he longed for ackee she would lick the ackee tree with the house broom and cook a heap. And if Ptolemy had thought to ask for the stars, I'm sure that good Mummy would probably have climbed a ladder with her old basket made of moss grass and gathered him a bundle of the most twinkling ones.

LAWD HAVE MERCY!

But the more Mummy did for Ptolemy the more spoiled he became, so that whenever she wasn't able to satisfy his every whim he would go into his shell and sulk. And nothing could vex Mummy Turtle more than that. Sometimes she would roll on her back and kick and holler "Lawd have mercy" right in the public lane. Only a strong cup of nerves tea could calm her down.

Now one day when the sun was hot enough to fry an egg, Mummy went to check her garden. As usual she spoke kindly to each plant so that each one would grow up strong and healthy. Her method always worked and no one could deny that Mummy Turtle had a fertile garden. Why, the watermelons, who loved flattery, grew like hippopotamuses.

A Glimpse of Aunt Fatty

"Marvellous," she uttered as she ambled around the largest one, examining it. "Aunt Fatty will be passing by for Sunday tea, and sliced watermelon will be a good pick-me-up." So she rolled it into the shade of her allspice house.

Ptolemy was playing cricket with a coconut bunker for a bat and a sour orange ball, when he saw the beautiful watermelon. He told his mother that he loved it better than his best friend Hoppy the Frog, his piggy bank, bubble gum, water pistols, and all manner of good things. He wanted some right then and there!

But Mummy Turtle smiled and said, "Son, you must wait patiently for Aunt Fatty Poke." (That was her full name as she was both fat and enormously slow.)

Well, Ptolemy went into his shell and sulked as hard as he could. However, this time Mummy remained calm, for this was a different day and things would have to be different on a different day, that was Mummy's simple logic.

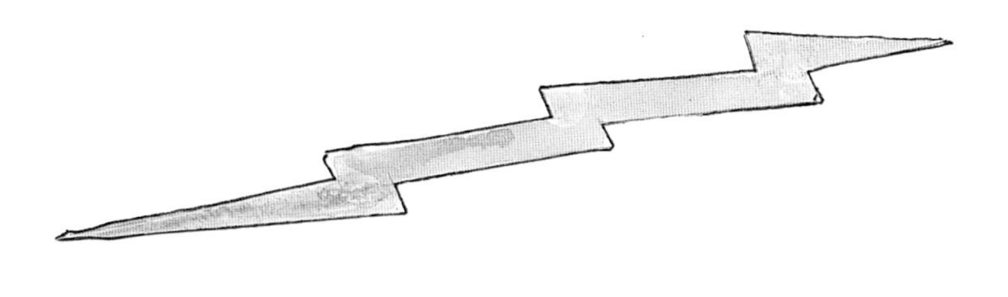

Ptolemy saw that Mummy wasn't in a hurry to please him, so he decided to run away from home. But he had never run before in his life (nor had any turtle, for that matter). So he just took serious strides down the public lane.

CLA CLA CLA CALAMITY!

He hadn't gone far when suddenly a squall developed and the clouds grew sinister and swollen and grey. The wind began to whip about like a cowboy's lasso. The rain rattled on leaves and roofs like the galloping of horses' hooves.

Mrs. Henpeck, a passerby, began to shout, "Cla cla, cla, calamity!"

"My umbrella!" cried a dreadful mongoose. "A moth tried to steal it!"

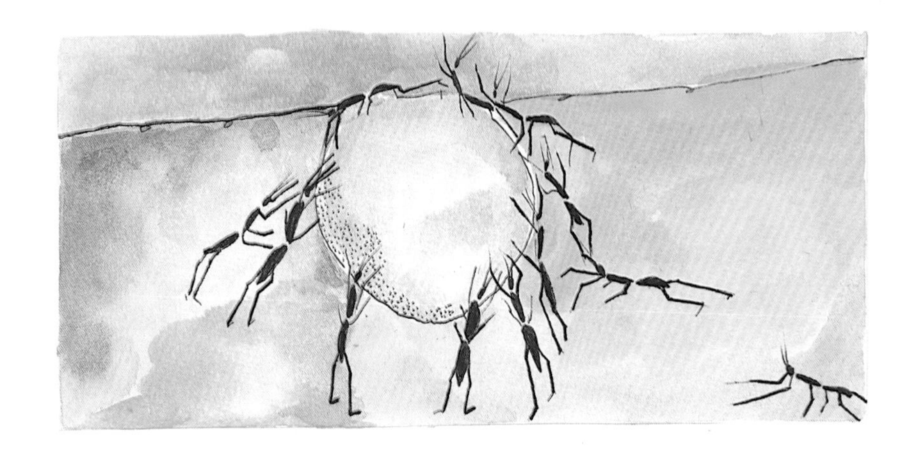

Donkey Oaty sent off his alarm like a rusty trumpet. A party of ants were panicking over a picnic crumb the size of a planet, and flowers were losing their heads, truly.

Ptolemy sought the shelter of a breadfruit tree and conveniently parked himself under it like a car. Just when he was feeling somewhat secure, the wind rudely shook the tree until a breadfruit fell directly on his head.

Ptolemy got the “Bump-On-The-Head” sickness. He saw stars bursting in space and then he began to dream.

Right away all the rain turned a lovely pink with black polka dots. Ptolemy tasted a puddle and it was the sweetest rain the sky had ever made. He had a lavish shower in it, splashed in it and drank it. He was full of glee, for he realised that he was right in the middle of a watermelon rainstorm.

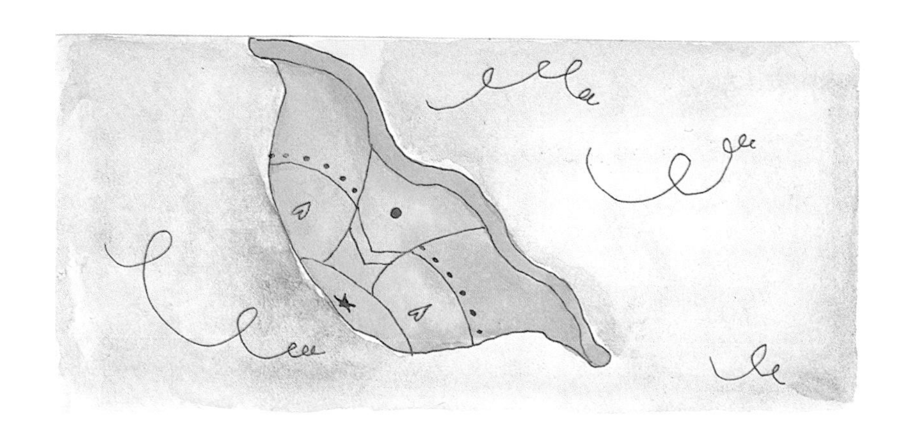

But the wind, who was terribly jealous of all other weather conditions and wanted to be king of the sky, blew like a bully, harder and harder until anything it disliked was blown out of sight.

Though Ptolemy held on for dear life with his long toe nails embedded in the earth, the wind blew the shell off his body and sent it sailing into outer space.

As Ptolemy watched it vanish he spotted a dozen angels jumping off the edge of a nearby nimbus cloud. They were a first-aid team coming to help victims of the storm.

Ptolemy's angel was pretty but he couldn't stare at her for the rays of her halo were blindingly brilliant. She wasn't a chatty angel either and spoke swiftly. "Follow me," she said. "The market is near – Watermelon Man will help you."

Well, Watermelon Man, whose very smile was like a generous curved slice of watermelon itself, amazed Ptolemy. His watermelons came in all sizes, from football to hippopotamus. The angel asked for one medium watermelon (cannonball size) and measured it to be sure it was just right. She then carved it in half with her cutlass (they come in handy in heaven too!).

She cleaned out all the fruit inside, dipped it in water to remove the sticky part and then placed one half right on Ptolemy's back.

"There," she said, "a new shell and all is well. Travel on before it is dawn."

There was no time to say thank you, for Ptolemy immediately blinked and returned to his usual self. There was a bump upon his head but all the rest had been just a dream.

I better do something before something do me, thought Ptolemy.

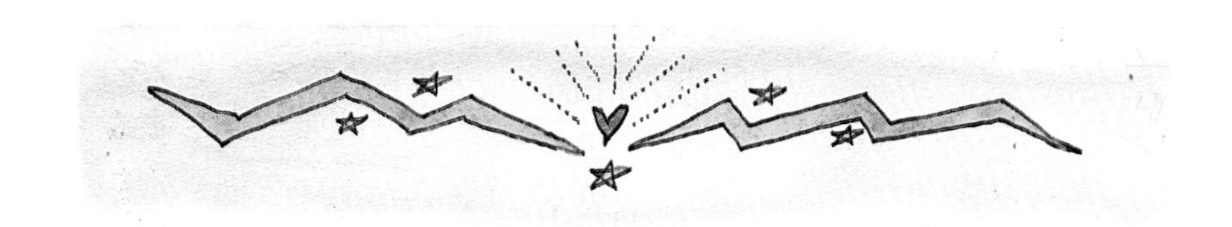

He reached home by a stream of moonlight. Mummy was waiting with a tapping foot, that meant, "Just where have you been all night, sir?"

But when she saw his swollen head, she got out her all-purpose lime juice cure, because she was a good Mummy who knew politeness and how to reason. She dabbed it and kissed it and wrapped it in a banana bandana.

Now, Aunt Fatty came and went and ate a great deal in between, and so there was only one watermelon slice remaining. But Ptolemy, who grew more grateful with each passing minute, accepted it with glee. Anyway, there was no room for sulking, at least not in his shell, not with a bump the size of a coconut, for his head would just not fit.

Mother and Son

Since Ptolemy did not sulk, Mummy could not get vexed, so all was well under that heavenly allspice tree.

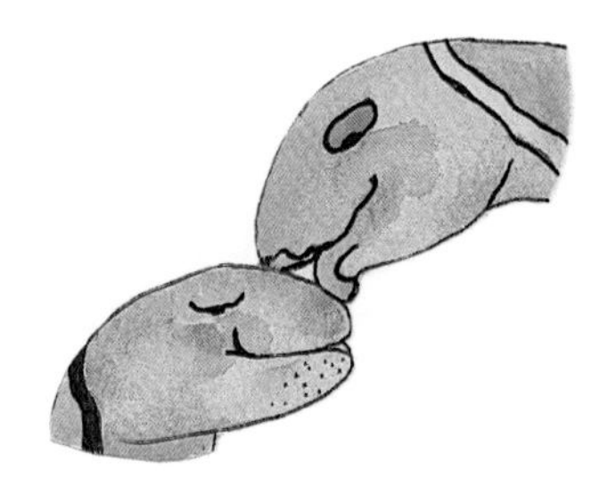

A Goodnight Turtle Kiss

FOOTNOTES
AND WORDS YOU MAY NOT KNOW

Ackee	The national fruit of Jamaica. It grows on a tree, in a red pod with large black seeds. The pale yellow meat inside must be cooked. When eaten with saltfish it is Jamaica's national dish.
Allspice	A tree with small berries used for spice when dried - also called pimento.
Banana Bandana	A wordplay meaning a banana leaf worn as a bandana or large scarf.
Blue Drawers	Cakes made of cornmeal, sugar and spices, wrapped in banana leaves and steamed.
Breadfruit	A tree that first came from Tahiti, brought by Captain Bligh in the eighteenth century. It has fingered leaves, and bears a large green fruit which has a texture like bread and can be eaten fried, boiled or roasted.
Cerasee	A vine that grows wild. The leaves can be boiled to make a green bitter tea which is good for cleansing the blood.
Coconut Bunker	A long piece of fibre that grows around the upper trunk of the coconut tree. It is stronger than bark and has a good shape for use as a baseball bat.

Cutlass	A short, heavy sword with a curved, single-edged blade good for cutting sugar cane and coconuts, for example. Also called machete.
Devil's Horsewhip	A weed with a whiplike stem that stings when brushed against. It is used as a herb to make tea.
Donkey Oaty	A wordplay that sounds like Don Quixote, a Spanish gentleman who was always trying to make wrong into right when it was impossible to do so.
Larynx	A part of the throat where the vocal cords are located, which is where the voice comes from.
Lasso	A long rope with a running noose at one end, used to catch cattle, horses, etc.
Lick	To lap up but also to thrash or hit - the meaning used in the story of Ptolemy.
Nerves Tea	A green tea of boiled soursop leaves.
Nimbus	A dark grey rain cloud (Latin).
Ptolemy	A Greek astronomer of the second century AD. Also any king of the dynasty which ruled Egypt from 323 to 30 BC. It is pronounced Tolemy which sounds good with Turtle.
Squall	A sudden violent gust of wind or brief turbulent storm.

Photo by Chloë Potter

Mélisande Potter-Hall began a performance career at the age of five. She has received many scholarships for her achievements in the fields of classical ballet, concert piano and art. In 1971 she wrote her first children's book, for which she received an Ingram Merrill literary award. She has since written many children's stories.

In 1973 she co-founded the Mystic Paper Beasts Theatre Company, which became internationally acclaimed for its mask and design ingenuity. One of the many plays which she wrote and designed during her theatre years - On The Ball, An Insect Drama was published by Fast Books (Taos, New Mexico) in 1984. Mélisande's performance art has been exhibited in major museums, galleries, theatres and festivals around the world.

In 1987 she arrived in Jamaica to perform for national television and to conduct a seminar in drama at the University of the West Indies. On touring the island professionally, she became enamoured with the vibrancy of nature's colours, the different way of life, and the agile grace of the people, and she decided to make the island her home.

Since then she has been focussing on her watercolour paintings (she is mainly self-taught) and has exhibited her works throughout the island, as well as in the USA and England. Ptolemy Turtle is her first Jamaican story, and was written while she resided in Windsor Castle, Portland, among country folk. As the story grew she would read a portion each evening to passersby along an old, unused railroad track.

Mélisande is married to Jamaican musician Michael Hall and lives between Ocho Rios and Rhode Island where she visits her daughters Chloë and Giselle.